Spy Cats 2

The Revelation

Amma Lee

Introduction

After they failed to save the President's daughter, Elizabeth Conrad; Bean and the Fury Three vowed to not let the same mistake happen twice! After receiving an anonymous tip from a mouse, Bean and the Fury Three learned that Mr. Hamster and his minions were holed up in an abandoned computer warehouse. Bean and Blue came up with a plan to infiltrate the facility; however, things take a turn that neither Bean nor Blue could have ever predicted.

Not only is the President's daughter in danger, but the whole human race as well. The Fury Three ends up in an unforeseeable situation that might require assistance from the evil mastermind, Mr. Hamster! "The Revelation" is a story that shows that everything isn't what it may seem and that anything can happen. Will Bean's determination to not let himself be held back because of his size be an asset or a major liability?

Chapter One

"Bean," Blue said, as he walked into Bean's office. Bean was working on his hacking skills since it was apparent that hacking into things would become an integral part of his job. The Abyssinian cat looked up at the cougar who had a grave expression on his face.

"Good morning, Blue," Bean said with a slight smile on his face. It was still early in the morning, so the smaller cat still felt a bit sluggish. "How's everything going? Any leads on where Mr. Hamster went?" A few days ago Mr. Hamster had gotten away after Bean had saved the Fury Three from their imprisonment at the old garbage facility. However, even though Bean managed to save the Fury Three, they failed in saving the President's daughter, who had been their primary mission.

Blue shook his head and sighed.

"No, but I'm sure one of us will find some trace of Mr. Hamster soon." Blue walked around Bean's desk then to see what he was doing. Bean could tell that Blue was still upset that his plan had failed and that his plan ended up getting the Fury Three captured. No matter how many times the unit told Blue that mistakes happens, Blue was still unable to shake the feeling of defeat.

The sorrow that was coming from Blue made Bean feel sorry for the larger cat.

"It's alright, Blue," Bean whispered. Bean knew that Blue didn't want to talk about it any longer, so that was the only comfort he allowed himself to give Blue. Blue sighed again, but this time, he nodded his head in understanding.

"Thanks, I'll be alright." Blue cleared his throat and grabbed a remote control off of Bean's desk and pushed a button. "I am going to link my data to your hologram." Once the hologram's screen and the keyboard were displayed, Blue's paws rapidly typed some information into the hologram. Bean stopped what he was doing to give Blue his full attention.

"What's this program you're using?" Bean was assigned to work with Blue from now on, sort of like his protégé, so there were many things that he still needed to learn from Blue.

"This is the program that I use to search for individuals using whatever information that I've acquired from them." Blue typed in a few more things into the hologram and soon a picture of Mr. Hamster was displayed on the screen.

"Woah," Bean said in surprise at all of the information that showed on the screen. Blue had collected a lot of data on Mr. Hamster and it was a shame that they hadn't found him yet. Blue grinned at Bean then. Blue was always proud when someone was impressed with his work, it had taken him many years to become an expert at it.

"This is nothing," Blue said and pushed a button on the top left-hand corner of the screen. "I even know what he likes to eat and what music helps put him to sleep." To most people having that information was useless, but to Blue, any information about their enemies was useful information to have.

"We'll definitely find Mr. Hamster and his minions soon with this," Bean commented, nodding his head. Bean saw the determination that lit up in Blue's eyes, a determination that Bean hadn't seen since they had come home from their semi-failed mission.

"Of course, we will," Blue said in a matter a fact way. "The Fury Three are the best in the world after all," Bean smiled happily. He was happy that Blue was starting to get his confidence back.

"Blue! Bean!" The two cats quickly turned their faces to Bean's office door. Red was standing at the door with a grave expression on his face. Bean and Blue knew right away that something important had occurred.

"What's wrong, Red?" Blue said as he made his way over to the snow leopard. Red just shook his head.

"Not here, let's go to the conference room. Matthew and Green are waiting for us." Red didn't wait for Blue's or Bean's response as he immediately took off down the hallway.

"Shut the hologram down," Blue said and made a b-line after Red.

3

"Right," Bean said and quickly closed down the hologram. He didn't want the information to be seen by possible spies. The odds of someone breaking into the Fury Three's headquarters were extremely unlikely; however, they weren't going to take that chance and be proven wrong.

"Bean, hurry up and sit down!" Blue said once Bean had finally walked into the conference room. Bean was embarrassed that everyone was waiting for him before they began. Usually, they'd start the meetings without him, but since he was working with Blue now, they absolutely needed everyone at the meeting.

"Let's start," Matthew said as soon as Bean took his seat. "An anonymous person tipped us off to the whereabouts of Mr. Hamster and the President's daughter," Matthew said, wasting no time in getting straight to business.

"That's great news," Bean said absentmindedly and immediately closed his mouth once he felt everyone's eyes on him. Bean had a habit of talking out of turn whenever they learned something new. Matthew gave Bean a stern look before nodding his head.

"Yes, that is excellent news," Matthew pushed a button that was on the podium that he stood behind. The image that displayed on the screen was an image that Bean had seen in an old history book. Bean remembered reading about buildings that specialized in making what humans called 'computers.'

Bean was dying to comment on the computer warehouse, but he'd wait until the end. He wanted to show Matthew and the Fury Three that he could be as equally as mature as them. "This is what was known as a computer warehouse. When computers and laptops were prominent hundreds of years ago, this was one of the buildings that these 'computers' were created in." Matthew pushed a button and zoomed in on the building. "Some of our spies came across a little mouse who offered this information to us, this mouse wished to be anonymous so we won't be able to thank him for this information if it's correct."

"We should head there right away," Green, the mighty cheetah, said. "I owe that little hamster a knuckle sandwich for what he did to me!" Green growled as he remembered being overtaken by one of Mr. Hamster's robots. Green thought heavily on that since then, and he vowed to make Mr. Hamster pay for making him look like a weakling.

"In due time, Green. Please relax." Matthew said. The Fury Three were not about revenge and he'd never allow his team to act on hate. Saving the President's daughter in stealth was the way that Matthew preferred the team to take on this mission. If at all possible, he'd like to rescue the girl and detain Mr. Hamster without fighting.

Green sighed. He knew that Matthew wasn't going to let him go in swinging like the angry cheetah that he was. Instead of whining further about the situation, Green listened to the details of the mission in silence.

"Alright, please review all of the details," Matthew said and then looked at Bean and Blue. "Let's make a plan that will without a doubt succeed!"

"Sir!" Bean and Blue said and watched as the Bengal left the room.

"We're counting on you," Red said as he and Green exited the conference room after Matthew. Blue turned towards Bean then and grinned.

"Alright rookie, let's get things started." Bean nodded his head enthusiastically. He was ready to take on this task with Blue.

Chapter Two

Bean watched as Blue sat with his eyes closed in deep meditation. Bean thought that they'd be bouncing ideas off of each other. He would have never thought that this was what they were going to do.

"Umm…" Bean stammered out confused. What exactly was he supposed to be doing here?

"Silence… I need to concentrate." Blue said with his eyes still closed.

"Uh… right, sorry." Bean didn't know why he was apologizing. If they were supposed to be working together, why wasn't Blue letting him in on what he was thinking? After what seemed like hours had passed, Blue finally opened his eyes and pushed a button on his desk, which made a hologram screen come up.

"Come closer, Bean," Blue said as he began typing on the

keyboard.

"Right!" Bean chirped. He was overjoyed at finally being included into whatever Blue was thinking about. "How can I assist you?" Bean asked, waiting for Blue to give him instructions.

"I want you to watch how I map out my plans," Blue said as he turned on the same program that Bean had shown him earlier. It didn't take Blue much time to type in his plan, and soon his plan had a life.

"What is this?" Bean asked as he watched a holographic Fury Three infiltrating what Bean believed to be a computer warehouse.

"This my little cat friend is the reason why my plans always work," Blue said with a big smile on his face. "I plan how the Fury Three will navigate the grounds of our mission and in turn this program shows me how successful it's going to be."

"Really?" Bean didn't know that programs were capable of doing that. On paper, the way that Blue came up with plans was bulletproof, but it didn't take into consideration on what the enemy could do. "But... this doesn't really show you what the enemy has up their sleeves." Blue nodded his head in agreement.

"Right, I am working on a program that could determine that, but right now it isn't up and running. I generally think of several things that could happen and input each of those possibilities in. I'm usually correct, but..." Blue trailed off then obviously thinking about their last mission. "Anyways, this is where you'll come in," Blue said, and Bean understood that Blue wanted Bean to give him a list of some things that could possibly happen.

"Right, you want my opinion on things that might happen, right? Give me a few minutes." Bean said, and the room got quiet then. Bean knew that Mr. Hamster had researched more ways to counterattack the Fury Three and other government officials who might be out to get him. Bean thought long and hard about what he had noticed on their last mission. "Come on, Bean," Blue said, irritated. He wasn't used to working with someone on making a plan, so the fact that he had someone else doing the thinking instead of himself made time go by so much slower.

"Robots," Bean said looking over at Blue, who had a confused expression on his face. "Mr. Hamster used advanced and powerful robots in our last battle. There's no reason to think that he wouldn't use them again. I'm also pretty sure they'd be stronger." Blue nodded his head, finally understanding where Bean was going with that.

"Alright, any idea on how to counterattack a more powerful robot?"

"Well… Robots will have a weakness and a power switch. If we're up against them, I believe we could turn them off." Bean knew that the information was pretty basic, but that was a start. Blue moved his whiskers quickly as if thinking about what Bean had said before typing it into his planning program.

Bean believed that nobody would ever match Blue when it came to planning and coming up with a strategy, especially not him. The Fury Three commented that Bean was good at planning; however, most of his planning came on the fly of the moment. No matter how much preplanning one did, Bean actually believed that events would happen that were not a part of their initial plan.

"Okay, any other suggestions," Bean told Blue his thoughts as they came to mind and soon the two cats had enough information to come up with an initial plan, and a few backup plans if the first plan failed. "Alright, let's head back," Blue said with a sense of accomplishment running throughout his body.

The two cats made their way to Matthew's office. Matthew lifted his head once the two cats arrived.

"Have you two figured something out?" Matthew asked once again getting straight to the point.

"Yes, we have," Blue said exposing his sharp teeth in a happy grin. Matthew nodded his head and looked at Bean.

"Go round up everyone," Matthew said, and Bean smiled as well.

"Sir," Bean quickly went to Red's and Blue's office, and they walked to the conference room together. Once they were there, Red, Green, and Matthew took their seats while Bean and Blue took to the podium.

"Bean and I came up with a bulletproof plan that'll surely work!" Blue always said that about his plans, and other than their last mission, his plans normally did work.

The two stood up at the podium and told the group exactly what they were going to do and how they were going to get into the former computer warehouse. Red, Green, and Matthew were incredibly impressed by the plan. More specifically, they were impressed by the young Bean. Bean spoke of the scheme with such expertise despite the fact that this was the first time that Bean had collaborated with Blue to come up with a plan for a mission.

"Any questions?" Matthew asked and looked around the room. "Get to work!" Matthew said once everyone shook their heads no.

"So when are we going?" Green asked impatiently. Bean answered the cheetah right away.

"Now, Blue and I feel that we have given Mr. Hamster too much time to re-plan. We need to stop him now before he makes his army of robots and regular hamsters stronger."

"Good thinking," Red said, patting Bean on the head. This made the smaller cat angry, but he didn't say anything because he knew that Red meant well. "Did our shipment come in today?" Red asked turning towards Green whose office was closer to where all of their things were delivered.

"Yes and I saw four packages instead of three," Green said and looked at Bean. Green thought that Bean was capable enough to accompany them on their missions. As long as Bean left the fighting to Green, then there was nothing for the Abyssinian cat to worry about.

"What packages?" Bean asked curiously. He didn't know that the team was ordering something for him as well.

"Invisibility suits," Blue said, running out of the room and then coming back in with a box in his mouth. He ripped the box opened quickly and pulled out a weird looking outfit. "I've ordered these as a precaution for when we met up with Mr. Hamster again," Blue said as he carefully put on the black suit.

"It looks like a costume for human children," Bean commented about the outfit that Blue had put on. Animals were required to wear clothes as well once they started to co-inhabit the world with humans as their equals, but animals had unique clothing that looked much more different than humans' clothes. This suit, however, screamed human.

"These were the only ones in stock, so these will have to do," Blue said and pushed a button on his suit. In a matter of seconds, the cougar was completely invisible.

"Woah!" Bean shouted in surprise. He's seen pictures of high-tech invisibility suits; however, this was his first time seeing one up close and personal.

"Alright, everyone suit up," Red said as he walked to the other room to get his invisibility suit. Bean's paws were getting sweaty because of how nervous he was, but he knew in his heart that this time they would be successful.

Chapter Three

"This is it," Blue said as the four cats landed on the outside of the computer warehouse grounds. Bean scanned the area for enemies, and there were some, but it wasn't heavily guarded like the garbage dump was.

"It's strange," Red mumbled then. "Why aren't there many patrol robots around?" Red said as he looked from side to side making sure that none of the robots were coming their way. He didn't want them to get captured like last time, so Red made it his mission to look out for the mighty robots. "Maybe we should use our invisibility suits."

"Maybe that hamster hadn't had enough time to build more of them," Green said cracking his paws. "No matter, though, he can have a whole army of those robots, and he'd never take me down." Green made a vow to himself to never be pushed to the side like some typical back alley cat ever again.

"I don't know about that, also I don't think these suits would work on a robot." Bean said. It was strange that Mr. Hamster didn't have a lot of patrol outside, but Bean didn't think it was because Mr. Hamster didn't have enough patrol robots at the moment. Bean was sure that the robots were more advanced and powerful than before. "Get down!" Bean said quickly and lowered his body to the grassy plain. The others followed Bean quickly and stood as still as possible.

"No threat detected." A robotic voice could be heard. Just then they saw a large robot flying over them with a large light barely missing the spot where they were crouched down at. Mr. Hamster had developed flying robots!

"Tsk! I knew it!" Bean hissed once the coast was clear. Bean figured that Mr. Hamster would make his robots stronger and more advanced, but making them fly was something that even he hadn't considered being possible in such a short length of time.

"We must hurry!" Red said and got up on all fours. "We must get inside of the building as soon as possible. We do not need to be hunted by that." The Fury Three and Bean knew that Red was right. If those robots could fly, they were probably stronger as well.

"I'll try to find an opening," Bean said and quickly pushed the button on his remote control to pull up his hologram. He didn't know how often the hamster-bots patrolled the area, so he wanted to find the easiest and safest way into the building as soon as possible. It took Bean a few moments, but he located an opening not too far from their position.

"Get down!" Red whispered again as he saw another robot flying to their destination. The four quickly lowered their bodies to the ground.

"Suspicious sounds in this area," the robotic voice said, and Bean shivered in fear. *Not again*, the Abyssinian cat thought as he feared that they'd be captured. The hamster's light shined on the grass for several seconds before looking in front of it. "False alarm, no intruders detected." They needed to be as far from that position as possible!

"This way," Bean said and crawled through the grass. Bean had a slight advantage navigating through the grass given how small that he was. The Fury Three took shorter steps since their massive bodies bobbing up and down could easily be detected. Soon the four were at the back door.

"I'll scan the other side for enemies. Bean, hack into the system so that we can get inside and hurry!" Blue said, wasting no time in his task.

"Right!" Bean said and quickly looked for ways to decode the security system. Mr. Hamster's security had gotten harder to crack, but Bean wouldn't let this get the best of him.

"Hurry up guys, that robot's coming back!" Red said. With his excellent line of vision, Red could easily see the robot quickly approaching them.

"Don't worry, Red," Green said getting into a defensive stance. "If that thing gets anywhere near us, I'll make it wish it never messed with the Fury Three!" Green was combat ready!

"No need I got it!" Bean said, and the doors' security system was disabled.

"There're no enemies directly behind this door," Blue said and quickly pushed the door opened. Blue couldn't stand the embarrassment of being captured again, so he was going to do anything in his power to make sure that wouldn't happen. Bean saw the robot move in closer to them as soon as they closed the door behind them.

As soon as their breathing had gone back to normal, Red faced his teammates.

"Alright Blue, since you mentioned that splitting up would be in our best interest, you take Bean and Green and I will stick together." Bean wasn't initially with Blue's idea of splitting up the team, but after a lot of thought, he believed it to be a good idea. They'd be able to cover more ground that way.

"Sir!" the three shouted, and Red opened the door to make sure that nothing was guarding it.

"Green and I'll cover the left side, you two cover the right." With that said, they were gone.

"Come on, Bean. We should be able to find some information about what Mr. Hamster is planning. If we come across the girl, we'll contact them as soon as possible." Bean nodded his head, and the two crouched low to the ground making sure to be out of the enemies' line of vision.

****

Bean and Blue searched the right side of the building from top to bottom in search of Mr. Hamster's plans or the President's daughter without any success.

"Look up ahead!" Bean said as they neared a massive door. The door wasn't heavily guarded, but from the looks of it, the contents of the room had to have held some valuable information.

"I don't see any of those robots around, let's see what that hamster is hiding." Blue and Bean made their way to the door, and much to their surprise the door was open! They looked down the hall one more time before Blue scanned the inside of the room for enemies. "There's nothing or nobody inside." Without hesitation, Blue opened the door.

Bean glanced around the room that had many old computers on desks. All of the objects in there looked so old and exciting that Bean couldn't help but to look on in interest. He'd love to see how these 'computers' used to work.

"What the?" Blue said all of a sudden and Bean blinked rapidly as he was brought back to the situation at hand. Bean could barely see that Blue was fumbling around with some information that he pulled up on his hologram. Bean's heart was beating fast as he walked over to the cougar.

"What's wrong, Blue? What are you looking at?" The curious Abyssinian cat asked. Bean stood alongside Blue looking at the words that rapidly displayed on the screen.

"I found Mr. Hamster's plans and it doesn't look good!" Bean's eyes widened at that, and he too started to read the information that was displayed on the hologram. They honestly should have just taken the information and went to search for the President's daughter, but they were glued to their spots.

Mr. Hamster had been working on a formula to use to experiment on humans to turn humans into animals, and it appeared that Mr. Hamster wanted to use Elizabeth Conrad as his test subject! This information angered Bean. He wouldn't allow Mr. Hamster to accomplish his goals.

"Where is he keeping this formula?" Bean asked. Blue was reading so fast that it was almost impossible for the small cat to keep up.

"Mr. Hamster has been unsuccessful with his previous batches that he'd made before kidnapping the girl. It looks like he's in the process of making a new batch. These ingredients, though…" Blue paused and shook his head in disbelief. "Let's just say this isn't some concoction that humans should drink.

As Blue told Bean exactly what he was reading, Red's face appeared on the screen.

"We need your help! We've found the President's daughter, but some hamster-bots have caught on to us!"

"We're coming now!" Without thinking, Bean ran out of the room and took off towards the direction of Red and Green. Bean knew that he should have waited for Blue, but Bean was sure that Blue was right behind him. Normally Blue would have been right behind him, but since the Fury Three was now discovered in the facility, all of the robots would make their way to Red and Green.

"I'll try to research this a little more before I lend them my strength," Blue said and this time he thoroughly read what Mr. Hamster was up to.

Chapter Four

"Red! Green!" Bean shouted as he came running into the room. The fight had already started, and the snow leopard and cheetah were dodging attacks from a flying robot.

"I'll take you down!" Green yelled as he made a dash for the robot, but the robot dodged Green's attack and shot a laser beam in his direction. Red pushed him out of the way before it made contact with the overly angry cat.

"It took you long enough," Red said and quickly took his eyes off of the enemy. "Where's Blue?" Red asked with a frown forming on his furry face. Bean turned to look behind him and was shocked to see that Blue hadn't followed him. The situation they were in was dire, and they really need the assistance from Blue because unlike Bean, Blue was able to handle himself against strong enemies in battle.

"I'm... I'm sure he's coming right now!" Bean shouted. Blue had to come because Bean was sure that he wouldn't abandon the Fury Three in their time of need.

"Intruder alert! Intruder alert! The Fury Three has been caught on the premises!" The robotic hamster said in a monotone voice.

"Tsk! It can't be helped. Bean, figure out a way to open that cage device that the girl is in! Green and I will handle this robot!" Bean looked towards the back of the room and finally noticed Elizabeth Conrad! She was enclosed in some type of see through cage, and she was banging on it and screaming words that he couldn't hear.

"Right!" Bean said and made his way towards the back of the room.

"Not so fast!" A voice called out, and Bean knew immediately who it was before he even saw him. It was Mr. Hamster! "You ruined my plans a few days ago; however, I don't plan to let you ruin these plans now." Mr. Hamster said and laughed right before pushing a button to close the doors to the room.

"Tsk! Let the human go, Mr. Hamster! I won't let you hurt this girl!" Bean wouldn't let Mr. Hamster see his dreams come true.

"Humph! I will see my dreams come true, and I will make all of these pathetic humans pay!" Mr. Hamster said and made a dash towards Bean. Mr. Hamster usually allowed his minions to fight for him, but this time, he wanted to be the one to defeat the Fury Three and Bean. Bean immediately got into a fighting stance and made a b-line towards Mr. Hamster.

"Ah!" Bean's battle cry resonated through the room, and he extended his claws when he got close to Mr. Hamster. The sound of their claws hitting each other was similar to the sound of cars crashing into one another. Bean always worked behind the scene, but this time, he was dead smack in the middle of a battle with the world's most evil mastermind.

"You're still fast as ever, Bean!" Mr. Hamster said, as he opened his furry cheeks to try to bite Bean. Bean dodged the hamster's sharp teeth and followed it up with a swipe of his paw. "Ugh!" Mr. Hamster groaned as Bean's paw connected with his cheeks and sent him flying back.

"You have to hurry, Bean!" Red called out as he and Green were still in a heated battle with the robot. The team looked exhausted, and Bean knew that he needed to figure out a way to disable the robot and beat Mr. Hamster at the same time. Just when Bean thought that, he saw a small device with a button fall from Mr. Hamster. Bean knew right away that it controlled the robot in the room.

"Here's my chance!" Bean yelled and ran towards the button. Still disoriented, Mr. Hamster tried to make it to it first!

"No!" Mr. Hamster cried out in vain. Bean was incredibly small, but at the end of the day, Bean was still fast. Bean pushed the button and as expected the robot stopped attacking.

"Way to go, Bean," Red said once the robot fell in front of him and Green. Green's eyes narrowed then as he turned them towards Mr. Hamster.

"Alright fur ball," Green said and crouched down low as if he was going in for the attack. "You're going to pay for that robot hitting me the other day," Green said and leaped into the air.

"Eeek!" Mr. Hamster shivered in horror as the cheetah seized him.

"That's enough, Green!" Red shouted. This wasn't a mission for revenge, this was a rescue mission. "We're arresting him and taking him in for questioning," Red looked at Bean then. "Get that cage open, Bean. I doubt that this hamster would be kind enough to do that."

"Right," Bean went straight to work on getting the cage open and in no time the President's daughter was free. As soon as she wasn't locked up anymore, she fainted!

"Tsk... I'll get her," Green said irritably and walked over to the girl and pulled her onto his back.

"Remember... those other robots are still on patrol if they aren't outside this very door." Red said as he firmly gripped Mr. Hamster into his mouth. "How do we turn them off?" Red asked the hamster, and Mr. Hamster just laughed.

"Ha! I won't cooperate with you! I might have been caught today, but I'll be back!" Mr. Hamster laughed maniacally, and Green swiped him with his paw. Red glared at Green, but Green just smiled.

"I'll do my best to shut them down now while they can't get to us," Bean said and quickly pulled out his hologram. In the midst of their battle with the robot, Mr. Hamster, and saving the President's daughter, the fact that Blue had never came did not cross their minds.

****

"President Conrad, my team is working hard on rescuing your daughter. She'll be safe and sound as soon as possible." Matthew said as he spoke with the sorrow filled President.

"She better be safe, Matthew. I put her safety in the paws of animals over humans. I have a lot of faith in you, so please do not prove me wrong. Save my daughter!" the President disconnected then, and Matthew sighed. Matthew understood that the President was worried about his daughter, but in a way, her capture was his fault. If President Conrad had never experimented on Mr. Hamster, they wouldn't be in that predicament.

"They'll complete the mission this time," Matthew wasn't blaming the Fury Three for not saving the President's daughter in their last mission. Everything will not always go according to plan. He could tell that his team was frustrated by it, especially Bean who had promised that he'd rescue everyone.

"He's proving to be a great asset to the team," Matthew said as he thought about the Abyssinian cat. Bean had the determination that could trump even the biggest of cats. His skills with hacking and his speed were definitely beneficial on their last mission. Matthew knew with Bean working together with Blue that there was no way that the team would fail in rescuing Elizabeth.

Matthew got up from his seat then and paced around his office. Even though he believed the Fury Three would be victorious, he couldn't shake a sense of unease. Matthew stopped walking after hearing movement in his office.

"Who's there?" Matthew's authoritative voice resounded in the room. Matthew's eyes scanned the large room, but he couldn't find anyone. Just when he started walking towards the door, he was overtaken by several humans and hamsters. "Unhand me!" Matthew screamed just before he was tied up.

"Matthew, the Bengal leader of the Fury Three," One of the men said, looking down at the confused cat. "You're under arrest for conspiring and aiding in the kidnapping of Elizabeth Conrad."

"What? Conspiring! Kidnapping! I'm trying to save the girl!" Matthew yelled at the top of his lungs. How dare they arrest him on false accusations, this had to be some type of mistake, he was being framed!

"Struggling will only make things worse." The man said and allowed his men to take a hold of Matthew. The man walked around Matthew's office looking for anything that might be useful to him. He took Matthew's remote control and some items that outlined his previous mission. "Ah, this will be helpful to Dr. Z." He whispered under his breath.

"Those are confidential!" Matthew screamed as he noticed the man pocketing some valuable information. The mysterious man looked over at his comrades and nodded his head. Pulling out a remote control from his pocket, one of the men pointed it at Matthew's mouth. Soon enough, Matthew's mouth was closed shut.

"No more talking little kitty. You can talk all you want in Platinum Prison!" With that said, the mysterious individuals made their departure from the Fury Three's headquarters with Matthew as their prisoner.

Chapter Five

"Take him into his cell. I'll inform the boss of what's happening," Red said and made his way to Matthew's office.

"With pleasure!" Green said and quickly grabbed Mr. Hamster into his mouth before he had a chance to get away.

"I'll destroy you! I'll destroy you all once I'm free!" Mr. Hamster cried as he struggled in vain in Green's mouth. Bean listened to Mr. Hamster screaming as Green took him downstairs to the temporary jail that the Fury Three had at their headquarters. Bean was feeling good at that moment because they had succeeded in their mission.

"I'm glad that I was a part of this," Bean had beat himself up when he had failed at saving the girl before, but now he was grinning from ear to ear. Not only did they succeed in their rescue mission, but they also had succeeded in arresting Mr. Hamster! Bean was feeling fantastic at their accomplishments, but something in his stomach churned. He felt that something was still wrong, but he couldn't quite place his paw on what it might have been.

Bean decided to make his way back to his office to practice looking at the program that Blue had installed in his hologram controller, and that was when Bean realized why he was feeling a sense of dread.

"Blue!" Bean shouted. Through all of the commotion and confusion, the team had forgotten to search for Blue. Bean ran towards the door in search for his comrades, but immediately stopped in his tracks when Red came running towards him. The look on Red's face was a look that Bean had never seen on the leader's face. A look of complete devastation.

"Matthew has been taken!" Red said as soon as he saw the smaller cat. Bean's eyes went wide at that, and his mouth hung open in shock.

"How do you know this?" Bean wasn't one to question his superiors, but Red had to come across something that led him to believe that the administrator was captured.

"Matthew's office was trashed and many important files were taken," Red said and shook his head. "I also smelled several people in Matthew's room. Some were human and some were hamsters!

"Hamsters?!" Bean repeated. "Mr. Hamster has something to do with this I'm sure," Bean said confidently. Mr. Hamster was the only one who used hamsters to do his dirty work. Bean looked Red in the eye again once he realized that he had something to tell the larger cat as well. "Blue never joined us, I fear he's still at the computer warehouse."

"Tsk... I figured he'd catch up with us soon." Red said

shaking his head. Blue had never joined them in the battle so Red was sure it had something to do with the case, but this was unlike Blue. Not only did they have to find their boss, but they also needed to get in contact with Blue as well. The Fury Three wasn't complete without Blue!

"Blue? Blue are you there?" Red called out to his hologram. Red frowned when Blue hadn't responded back to him considering that he usually replied to Red as soon as he heard him. "What were you two doing before you came and found us?" Red asked, turning to Bean, who had a frown on his face as well.

"Blue and I found Mr. Hamster's plans, and it wasn't pretty," Bean said shaking his head once he remembered what he had read and what Blue had told him. "Anyways, when you called us for help, I left immediately, but I think Blue stayed behind."

"Do you remember where the room was?" Red asked. They needed to go back because they absolutely needed Blue to save Matthew.

"Yes," Bean said nodding his head quickly.

"Get ready, we're going to go back for him. Green will stay behind since we're in a desperate situation."

"Sir!" Red turned around and made his way to the prisoners' cells. Bean made his necessary preparation and waited for Red at the entrance. Bean knew that it was going to be a long and eventful day, but he hadn't expected for things to turn out like this.

****

Green wasn't thrilled to be left behind, but he understood the situation at hand and reluctantly agreed to keep Mr. Hamster out of trouble, and to make sure nothing else went wrong at the headquarters. Bean and Red were silent as they made their way back to the abandoned computer warehouse. The tension was noticeable, and Bean knew that both he and Red were wishing for the best.

"The robots should still be shut down, I don't think anyone would have been fast enough to get here if Mr. Hamster had reinforcements," Bean said more to himself than to Red. He was nervous, and the silence wasn't helping him at all. Soon the two cats were back at the computer warehouse and for the most part, nothing had changed.

"We need to get in and get out as soon as possible. We need to save the boss!" Red said as they both took off running once their paws touched the ground. It was much easier to navigate the building since there weren't any enemies around, so Bean and Red got to the room that Blue and Bean had found quickly.

"Blue!" Bean shouted Blue's name as soon as he opened the door. Much to their surprise, there was no sign of Blue anywhere. "Blue and I were in this room! This is where we found Mr. Hamster's plans." Bean started to walk towards the back of the room, but Red quickly stopped him by putting his paw up to block Bean's path.
"Look," Red murmured, and Bean followed Red's glance. Bean scanned the area and noticed that many of the old computers had been thrown to the ground and that the room, in general, was messier than the way that he left it. It didn't take Bean long to figure out what Red was thinking.

"You don't think that Blue was captured do you?!" *Not again…* Bean had just saved the Fury Three. Bean felt like all of his efforts were now in vain. Red didn't say anything as he made his way around the room in search of any clues. Bean watched Red silently, too shaken up to say anything.

"This is Blue's," Red said as he picked up Blue's remote control. Bean was surprised that the cougar had dropped it, just like Bean, Blue was never seen without it. Red turned it on quickly and gasped at the words that displayed on the screen.

Team,

If you are reading this, there is a high chance that I was captured. After Red had sent out his call for help, Bean rushed out immediately, but I stayed behind to continue reading the information that I've found. I hear those stupid hamster robots wreaking havoc outside the room, so I'll make this quick. Mr. Hamster is planning on turning all humans into animals to give everyone the pain that he felt when the government experimented on him. Bean and I found the ingredients that Mr. Hamster was concocting, and he was going to use Elizabeth Conrad as his test subject. I've destroyed it! Those ingredients would be the end of all humanity. My dear friends, I fear that we only know part of the story. I don't think Mr. Hamster is working by himself. He's referencing a scientist by the name of Dr. Z several times in his notes. I've found information regarding this Dr. Z, and I've come to the conclusion that Mr. Hamster is a victim in all of this as well! I wish I could tell you more about my findings, but those hamster-bots heard me and are breaking down the door! Those robots are not the brightest, so I'm sure that this information would get to you alright. Bean… it's up to you to read between the lines and research more into this.

Blue.

Red snarled after he read the last sentence. There was without a doubt that Blue was captured as well.

"Maybe we should search the facility. They might still be here!" Bean said. He didn't believe that Blue and the people who captured him would still be there, but he had to research all possibilities.

"It's no use. They're probably gone by now." Red said and looked at Bean with determination on his face. "It's time we head back to the headquarters. There's a certain hamster that we need to interrogate."

Chapter Six

Red burst into the headquarters doors without a care in the world. He had one objective at that moment, and that was to find out more information from Mr. Hamster. Bean had never seen Red so angry before, but it wasn't like he didn't have a good reason to be angry. Both of his close friends were captured, and it was all thanks to Mr. Hamster and his need for revenge.

"Where's Blue?" Green asked as soon as he saw Bean and Red. Red shook his head. Green would hear everything that he needed to know soon enough. Green looked over at Bean silently asking what happened, but Bean shook his head as well. The snow leopard did not want to go into too many details at the moment, so Bean didn't want to go behind Red's authority and provide Green with this information now.

"Hamster!" Red's voice came out in a roar. Mr. Hamster looked up and stared at Red with an unreadable expression on his face.

"So the cats have come back, are you here to question me? I'll tell you nothing!" Mr. Hamster said disobediently. Red pulled opened the locked cell with all of his might and walked over to Mr. Hamster, who started to tremble in fear. Even though he was scared, Mr. Hamster still wasn't planning on providing the Fury Three with any answers.

"What have you done with our leader and teammate?" Red asked. Mr. Hamster was going to give him answers even if he needed to force it from him.

"I've done nothing, as you can see I'm at this dreadful establishment with you." Mr. Hamster was still shaking; however, he didn't allow his fear to show in his voice.

"What did you do with our team before you got arrested?" Bean asked. Mr. Hamster looked over at the Abyssinian cat and frowned. Mr. Hamster was still bitter about losing to such a tiny cat.

"Like I said I don't know, and even if I did I wouldn't tell you," Mr. Hamster said and moved away from the angry cat. Green decided to enter the cell then. Green could see that Red was getting worked up, and Green couldn't have Red having all of the fun. Green snarled showing his sharp teeth to the hamster.

"Want me to give him a knuckle sandwich? That'll get this little fur ball talking." Green asked, and Red didn't immediately respond to that.

"Fine," Red said and moved out of the way. Bean couldn't believe that Red had agreed to that.

"No!" Bean shouted and ran in front of Mr. Hamster. He

32

wasn't defending the mastermind or anything like that, but Bean knew Mr. Hamster. He was stubborn and no matter what dangerous situation he was end, he wouldn't listen to anyone that demands things from him. "May I see Blue's remote?" Bean figured that Mr. Hamster would start talking if he was aware that he was being used as well.

Red and Green frowned, but Red threw the remote to Bean. Bean pulled up the information that Blue acquired and showed the screen to Mr. Hamster.

"We know what your plans were, Mr. Hamster. You planned on creating a formula and testing it out on the President's daughter to see if it'll turn her into a defenseless animal right?" Mr. Hamster's eyes widened at that, but he wasn't going to back down.

"Humph, I have no idea what you're talking about." Bean figured he'd say as much so he continued on as if Mr. Hamster had admitted to Bean's accusations.

"Okay, but did you know the scientist by the name of Dr. Z, the man who you've been working with behind the scenes, is using you and planning on turning on you as soon as possible?" This caught Mr. Hamster's attention, but he wasn't going to bite the bait just yet.

"What's all of this?" Green asked. Green caught on quickly that Blue must have been captured, but he had no idea about this other nonsense that Bean was talking about. Bean turned to Green then with a serious expression.

"Blue left us a holographic message before he was taken," Bean typed a few words into the keyboard and Blue's message appeared on the screen. Mr. Hamster didn't waste any time reading it as Bean explained what was going on. "Blue found some information about this Dr. Z in Mr. Hamster's plan and was able to hack Dr. Z's system. Whatever Blue found had led him to believe that Dr. Z is going to betray Mr. Hamster!"

"This must be a trap that your little teammate set up. He wanted me or my minions to find this note to raise suspicion in my ranks. It won't work, unfortunate for you." Mr. Hamster gave a small laugh. He didn't want this information to be accurate because if it were that would mean that he was naïve.

Bean looked at Mr. Hamster again and shook his head.

"I don't believe this to be the case, Mr. Hamster. You're a smart animal, why not look for the truth yourself?" Bean was being bold with his statements, but he had to do something before Blue and Matthew were lost forever.

"What are you doing?" Red asked. Red didn't remember giving Bean any rights to call any shots. He was a great asset to them, but at the end of the day, Bean was not one of the Fury Three. Red was the leader until they were able to rescue Matthew. Bean ignored Red because he had Mr. Hamster right where he wanted him. Bean knew what buttons to push just like Mr. Hamster knew what buttons to push.

"To find out for yourself; however, you'd need to work with us to find Matthew and Blue!" Bean knew that Mr. Hamster enjoyed acquiring knowledge of anything that he found interesting. Since Mr. Hamster might be a pun in a game he believed to be the king in, Bean knew that Mr. Hamster had no other choice but to accept Bean's proposal.

Red could see then what Bean was trying to do, and he had to admit that he was impressed by the cat. Red himself wouldn't have thought about that. Since Mr. Hamster worked with this 'Dr. Z' person, Red was sure that Mr. Hamster could give them enough information to find Dr. Z, Blue, and Matthew.

Mr. Hamster moved his whiskers back and forth in deep thought. He wouldn't let anyone take advantage of him, especially not a human. He'd help the Fury Three find their little companions, and he'd take down Dr. Z as soon as he verified that Blue's information was correct. He would not lose or be played with!

"Fine, let me out of here and I'll help you as much as possible with your little rescue mission." Mr. Hamster said. As soon as he was done taking care of business, Mr. Hamster would take down Bean and the Fury Three as soon as they let their guard down. Bean grinned, showing his smaller sharp teeth.

"Great!" Bean said and looked over at Red and Green with an apologetic expression on his face. He knew that he shouldn't have made a deal like this without their consent, Bean wasn't one of them, but he felt like this was the best route to go. Green looked displeased by the arrangement that Bean had made, but he'd have to go along with it if Red said so.

"This is on your head, Bean. Since you feel that you can make these decisions on your own, then you better come up with a bulletproof plan!" The steel in Red's voice wasn't lost on Bean, but Bean was confident that he'd be able to pull it off.

Never in his wildest dreams would Bean have thought he'd be working with his enemy, but that was the hand that was dealt for him. Mr. Hamster was the key to this mission, and he knew that Red understood that. Bean would make the Fury Three proud, and they will save Blue and Matthew. Mr. Hamster will help them shed light on this new revelation. Bean looked Mr.

Hamster in his eyes then, and the hamster gave a sinister grin.

"Alright, Mr. Hamster... tell us everything that you know."

Fin

CHARLIE
BOOK

Made in the USA
Middletown, DE
09 February 2023

24400213R00026